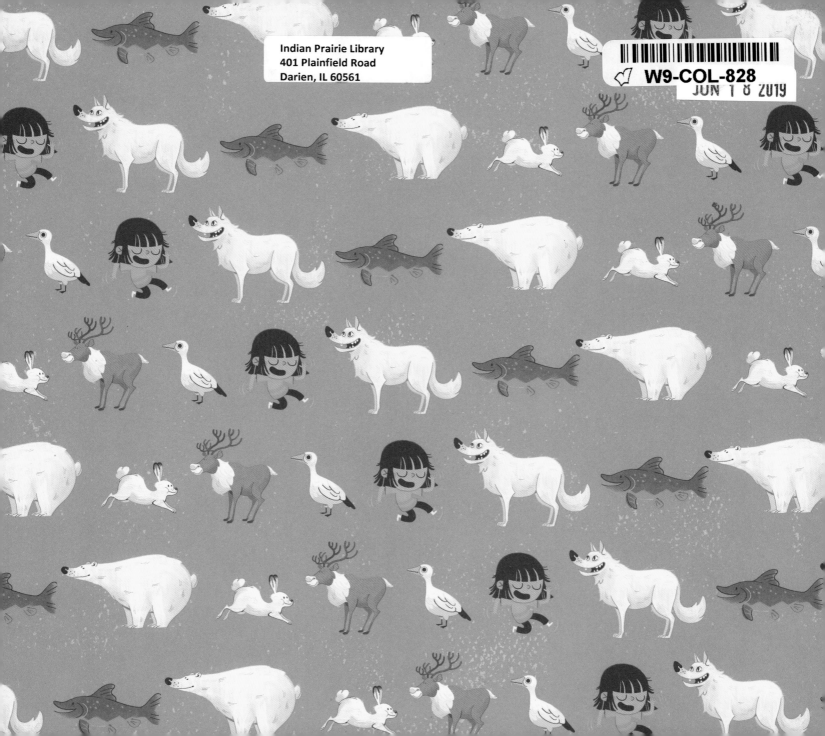

Published by Inhabit Media Inc.
www.inhabitmedia.com

Inhabit Media Inc. (Iqaluit) P.O. Box 11125, Iqaluit, Nunavut, X0A 1H0
(Toronto) 191 Eglinton Avenue East, Suite 310, Toronto, Ontario, M4P 1K1

Editors: Neil Christopher, Kelly Ward, and Kathleen Keenan
Art director: Danny Christopher

This project was made possible in part by the Government of Canada.

We acknowledge the support of the Canada Council for the Arts for our publishing program.

Printed in Canada

Canadä   Canada Council   Conseil des Arts
          for the Arts   du Canada

Library and Archives Canada Cataloguing in Publication

Mearns, Ceporah, 1986-, author
       It's time for bed / by Ceporah Mearns & Jeremy Debicki ; illustrated by
Tim Mack.

ISBN 978-1-77227-227-7 (hardcover)

       I. Debicki, Jeremy, author II. Mack, Tim, 1984-, illustrator III. Title.
IV. Title: It is time for bed.

PS8625.E27I87 2018   jC813'.6   C2018-904553-1

It's Time
For Bed

by Ceporah Mearns
& Jeremy Debicki

illustrated by
Tim Mack

Inhabit Media

It's time for bed. The sun has set.
Siasi, have you brushed your teeth yet?
NoooOOOooo! I don't want to brush my teeth!
I want to dance with the polar bear!
Roar, roar, roar!

2

It's time for bed. The sun has set.
Siasi, have you put on your PJs yet?
NoooOOOooo! I don't want to put them on!
I want to run with the caribou!
Run, run, run!

It's time for bed. The sun has set.
Siasi, have you put away all your toys yet?
NoooOOOooo! I don't want to put them away!
I want to fly with the geese!
Honk, honk, honk!

6

It's time for bed. The sun has set.
Siasi, have you picked a good night story yet?
NoooOOOooo! I don't want to pick a story!
I want to howl with the wolves!
"Aoooo, aaoooo, aaaoooo!"

It's time for bed. The sun has set.
Siasi, have you climbed up into bed yet?
NoooOOOooo! I don't want to get into bed!
I want to hop with the rabbits!
Hop, hop, hop!

10

12

It's time for bed. The sun has set.
Siasi, have you closed your eyes yet?
NoooOOOooo! I don't want to go to sleep!
I want to swim with the fish!
Swish, swish, swish!

13

It's time for bed. The sun has set.
You've danced with the polar bears,
run with the caribou,
flown with the geese,
howled with the wolves,
hopped with the rabbits,
and swum with the fish.
Siasi, are you ready for bed yet?

16

Yes, I'm ready for bed. . . .
What are you waiting for?
Let's go to bed!

17

18

Ceporah Mearns and Jeremy Debicki

Ceporah Mearns is from Pangnirtung, Nunavut, and Jeremy Debicki is from Winnipeg, Manitoba, but they call Iqaluit, Nunavut, their home. They live there with their children, Siasi and Siloah. They enjoy cooking family dinners, visiting friends and family, going sliding, and spending time at their cabin. Siasi inspired this story by always coming up with so many things she needs to do when it's time for bed.

Tim Mack

Tim Mack cannot fly like a goose, gallop like a reindeer, or swim like a fish, so instead he draws those things. Tim is a Canadian-born illustrator living in Vancouver, British Columbia. He enjoys playing with colours and shapes and never misses an opportunity to swim in the ocean, though he still wishes he could swim as well as a fish.

Inhabit Media

Iqaluit · Toronto